L

# Pooh's Best Friend

# Disney's
## Winnie the Pooh First Readers

Pooh Gets Stuck
Bounce, Tigger, Bounce!
Pooh's Pumpkin
Rabbit Gets Lost
Pooh's Honey Tree
Happy Birthday, Eeyore!
Pooh's Best Friend

# DISNEY's
## A Winnie the Pooh First Reader
# Pooh's Best Friend

## Ann Braybrooks
ILLUSTRATED BY Tim Jones

Disney
PRESS

NEW YORK

First Edition

1 3 5 7 9 10 8 6 4 2

This book is set in 18-point Goudy.

Library of Congress Catalog Card Number: 98-73265

ISBN: 0-7868-4265-2

For more Disney Press fun, visit www.DisneyBooks.com

# Pooh's Best Friend

One fine spring day,

Winnie the Pooh

got to thinking about friends.

He had many friends.

But who was his *best* friend?

Could it be Owl?

Eeyore?

Or Rabbit?

Tigger?

Kanga?

Or Roo?

And what about Piglet?

Hmm, Pooh thought.

What is a best friend?

I think I shall ask everyone

in the Hundred-Acre Wood.

Pooh licked some honey
from a honeypot,
then headed outside.

First, Pooh asked Owl.

"Owl, what is a best friend?"

"My Great-Aunt Gabby once said,

'A best friend is someone

you can talk to about anything.'"

said Owl.

Pooh and Owl talked about
some things.
They talked about the weather
and Owl's relatives.
But Pooh and Piglet
talked about everything.
They talked about hunting
heffalumps and finding honey.
They talked about the best places
for a picnic.

Next, Pooh asked Rabbit.

"Rabbit, what is a best friend?"

"If you must know,"

replied Rabbit,

"a best friend is someone

who is unselfish."

Pooh liked Rabbit.

But was Rabbit as unselfish as Piglet?

Pooh remembered

all the unselfish things

that Piglet had done for him.

He let Pooh sit by the fire

in his favorite chair.

He gave Pooh the biggest slice

of huckleberry pie.

Next, Pooh asked Eeyore.

"Eeyore, what is a best friend?"

"I wouldn't know, Pooh.

But I suspect it's someone

who remembers your birthday."

Pooh wondered if Eeyore

had ever remembered his birthday.

Once Piglet had thrown

a party for Pooh,

complete with balloons and cake

and honey lemonade.

Next, Pooh asked Tigger.

"Tigger, what is a best friend?"

"Hoo-hoo-*hoo*! That's easy,"
Tigger said.

"A best friend is someone
who sticks around,
even if you bounce him
accidentally."

Hmm, Pooh thought.

I stick around Tigger

when he bounces me.

Then Pooh remembered all the times

that Piglet had stuck around.

Like the time Pooh

had forgotten

to meet Piglet

at the bridge.

And the time

that Pooh had eaten

Piglet's lunch by mistake.

Next, Pooh asked Kanga.

"Kanga, what is a best friend?"

"A best friend, Pooh dear,

is someone who is patient

and kind," said Kanga.

Pooh thought,

that sounds like Kanga.

But then Pooh thought
a little longer.

Kanga had also described Piglet.

Piglet was all of those things
and more.

Piglet was easy to talk to.

He was unselfish and loyal.

And he always remembered
Pooh's birthday.

As Pooh turned to go,

Roo squeaked,

"I know what a best friend is!

A best friend is someone

who asks you to play!"

"You're right, Roo," said Pooh.
"Thank you!"
At that moment, Pooh knew
who his best friend was—Piglet.

Pooh walked along the path
and thought of all the marvelous
things that he and Piglet
had done together.
He saw a daisy and picked it.

He hurried to Piglet's house

and thumped on the door.

"Hello, Piglet!" said Pooh.

"I brought you a daisy."

"How kind of you,"

said Piglet.

"Would you like a piece

of huckleberry pie?"

The two friends sat inside.

But this time, Pooh insisted

that Piglet sit by the fire

in the comfiest chair

and take the biggest piece

of huckleberry pie.

For if Piglet was Pooh's best friend,

Pooh wanted to be his.

# Join the Pooh Friendship Club!

*A wonder—filled year of friendly activities and interactive fun for your child!*

## The fun starts with:

- Clubhouse play kit
- Exclusive club T-shirt
- The first issue of "Pooh News"
- Toys, stickers and gifts from Pooh

## The fun goes on with:

- Quarterly issues of "Pooh News" each with special surprises
- Birthday and Friendship Day cards from Pooh
- And more!

Join now and also get a colorful, collectible Pooh art print

Yearly membership costs just $25 plus 15 Hunny Pot Points. (Look for Hunny Pot Points 🍯 on Pooh products.)

To join, send check or money order and Hunny Pot Points to:

Pooh Friendship Club
P.O. Box 1723
Minneapolis, MN 55440—1723

Please include the following information: Parent name, child name, complete address, phone number, sex (M/F), child's birthday, and child's T—shirt size (S, M, L)

(CA and MN residents add applicable sales tax.)

Call toll—free for more information
1-888-FRNDCLB

Fun for kids ages 3–8!

Help your child learn
MATH and READING
with a computer and
a silly old bear.

©Disney

# Disney's Learning Series on CD-ROM

your child on the path to success in the 100 Acre Wood,
ere Pooh and his friends make learning math and reading
Disney's Ready for Math with Pooh helps kids learn all the
ortant basics, including patterns, sequencing, counting,
beginning addition & subtraction. In Disney's Ready to
d with Pooh, kids learn all the fundamentals including the
habet, phonics, and spelling simple words. Filled with
aging activities and rich learning environments, the 100
e Wood is a delightful world for your child to explore
r and over. Discover the magic of learning with Pooh.

NEW! Disney's Learning Series

Once Again The Magic Of Disney Begins With a Mouse

# Wonderfully Whimsical Ways To Bring Winnie The Pooh Into Your Child's Life.

## Pooh FRIENDSHIP

Pooh and the gang help children learn about liking each other for who they are in 5 charming volumes about what it means to be a friend.

## Pooh STORYBOOK CLASSICS

These 4 enchanting volumes let you share the original A.A. Milne stories — first shown in theaters — you so fondly remember from your own childhood.

## Pooh PLAYTIME

Children can't help but play and pretend with Pooh and his friends in 5 playful volumes that celebrate the joys of being young.

## Pooh LEARNING

Pooh and his pals help children discover sharing and caring in 5 loving volumes about growing up.

**FREE***
**Flash Cards Attached!**
A Different Set With Each
*Pooh Learning* Video!
* With purchase, while supplies last.